CAUGHT IN THE ACT!

The bus moved slowly past Brice Park. Randi spotted some boys skating around the old basketball court. She leaned forward.

"Look, Kristi!" she called, pointing. "Those are the boys Woody played roller hockey with yesterday." She leaned out the window to wave. "Hey, guys!"

Kristi grabbed the back of her shorts. "Careful, Randi! You'll fall out!"

"I'll be fine," Randi promised. "Hey, guys! It's me—"

Suddenly she froze. There, in the middle of the crowd of boys—it looked like . . .

"What's wrong?" Kristi asked. "Are you okay?"

Randi hung out the window, staring. "I don't believe it," she said. But she couldn't mistake that red hair.

It was Woody! He wasn't at home feeling sick and awful. He was out!

Out playing roller hockey with the guys!

Don't miss any of the fun titles in the Silver Blades

FIGURE EIGHTS series!

SILVER BLADES

FIGURE EIGHTS

My Worst Friend, Woody

Effin Older

Illustrated by Marcy Ramsey

Created by Parachute Press, Inc.

A SKYLARK BOOK

NEW YORK • TORONTO • LONDON • SYDNEY • AUCKLAND

*Special thanks to Page McBrier for
her help in preparing this book.*

RL 2.6, 006–009

MY WORST FRIEND, WOODY

A Skylark Book / July 1997

This book is for all kids who love to skate.

1

A Whole Summer of Woody!

"What am I going to do, Anna? I'll be miserable all summer without you!" eight-year-old Randi Wong moaned. She glided along the ice at the Seneca Hills Ice Arena.

Randi and all the other members of the Figure Eights skating club were there, warming up for their Tuesday lesson.

"I'm only going away to camp for six weeks," Anna Mullen reminded her. "It's not like I'll be gone forever!"

Randi hung her head. Her long black braids fell in front of her face. Six weeks sure *seemed* like forever!

It's not fair, she thought. *I shouldn't have to spend the entire summer without my best friend.*

She frowned. "I wish you would just stay here with me instead of going away."

Randi's other friends, Woody Bowen and Kate Alvaro, skated up to them.

Woody skidded to a stop. Ice chips sprayed up from his skates. His baseball cap sat backward on his red hair. "Hey, Anna," he said. "When are you leaving for Camp I-Wanna-Go-Home?"

"It's Camp Wanago, silly," Anna corrected. "And I'm leaving tomorrow. I'm really excited. It sounds so cool. They have horseback riding and swimming and archery and—"

"My older cousin is a counselor at Camp Wanago," Kate interrupted. "She loves it. You'll have a great time!"

"I know," Anna said. "This will be the first summer I *don't* have to spend inside an ice skating rink."

Woody and Kate laughed. Anna's father ran the pro shop at the Seneca Hills rink, and Anna helped him. She was there almost every day, winter *and* summer.

Woody's mom worked at the rink, too. She was president of Silver Blades, a skating club for older kids. And Randi's oldest sister, Jill, had been a member of Silver Blades before she'd gone off to skating school in Colorado.

So Woody and Randi spent a lot of time at the rink, too. That's how Anna, Woody, and Randi got to be such good friends.

"Hey, there's Samantha," Kate said. She waved. "See you guys later!"

Kate took off to join Samantha Rivers, Frederika Hamilton, Max Harper, and Josh Freeman on the other side of the rink. Randi, Anna, and Woody skated along the edge of the ice together. Actually, Randi and Anna skated. Woody tried to *walk* around the ice on his toe picks.

"I'll be so lonely without you, Anna," Randi complained. "Who am I going to hang out with?"

"Hey! What about me?" Woody punched Randi's shoulder lightly. "*I'm* your friend. *I'll* be around all summer. You can hang out with me!"

"Cool!" Anna chimed in. "You guys will have lots of fun!"

"I guess." Randi sighed.

"There are a couple of really good movies out that we can go see," Woody suggested.

"And you and Woody can play miniature golf

sometimes," Anna added. "Just like we usually do, Randi."

"Yeah." Randi felt herself smile. This really *was* starting to sound like fun!

"And you can go to the arcade," Anna said to Woody. "Randi and I love to play Space Invasion together."

"And we always swim at the town pool!" Randi joined in. "And go to Super Sundaes in the mall for ice cream—"

"And don't forget Vinny's for pizza!" Anna interrupted.

"Yeah!" Randi said, growing excited. "I can do all those things with *you* instead of Anna. We can totally have a blast, Woody!"

"Wow," Woody said. He crinkled his nose. "It sounds like we'll be spending practically *every minute* together."

"I know." Randi grinned. "Just like Anna and I usually do. Won't that be *great*?"

"Well, I—" Woody started to say.

But Randi interrupted him. "Hey! Why don't we hang out at the park tomorrow? We can play catch and ride bikes!"

Woody's face brightened. "Yeah! That sounds cool!"

"Really!" Anna agreed. "Too bad I can't be there."

"Well, you can't," Woody teased. "You'll be too busy at Camp I-Wanna-Go-Home!"

"You are so goofy!" Anna gave Woody a push.

Woody flapped his arms. "Whoa! Watch out," he cried, pretending he was going to fall. He flung his legs apart and grabbed on to Randi's elbow.

Randi lost her balance and reached out for Anna. "Help!" she cried, laughing. Randi's arms and legs went flying. All three friends tumbled down in a heap.

Randi sprawled on the ice, laughing. Woody was so funny. She would miss Anna—but maybe a summer without her wouldn't be so terrible. After all, she could spend every day with her *other* best friend—Woody!

2

Randi Has a Plan

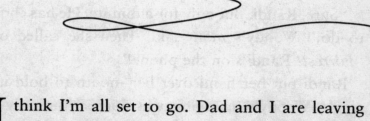

"I think I'm all set to go. Dad and I are leaving early tomorrow morning," Anna told Randi on the phone that night.

"Have fun at camp, Anna," Randi said. "Write to me if you can—and I'll write back."

"Okay," Anna replied. "Have fun at Figure Eights—and with Woody."

"I will," Randi promised.

She said goodbye and hung up the phone. She still felt sad that she wouldn't see her best friend until August.

But she was also excited about spending time with Woody!

Randi already had the best ideas for hanging out

this summer. She had figured out fun things to do every day for the next two weeks. And she couldn't wait to tell Woody about it!

Randi picked up the phone again. She punched in Woody's number. Mrs. Bowen answered, and Randi asked to speak with Woody.

"Sure, Randi. But only for a minute. He has chores to do," Woody's mom said. Then she called out, "*Forrest!* Randi's on the phone!"

Randi put her hand over her mouth to hold in a giggle. Woody's real name was Forrest. But only his mother called him that.

"Hey, Randi!" Woody said when he came to the phone. "What's up?"

"Go get a pencil and paper," Randi told him.

"Why?" Woody asked.

"So you can write down our summer plans," Randi answered.

"Huh? Why do I have to write them down?" Woody asked.

"So you won't forget, silly. There's a lot to remember. I planned out fun stuff for every day of the next *two weeks*!"

"Um . . . okay. There's a pencil and paper right

8

here by the phone," Woody told her. "I'm ready. I guess."

"Tomorrow we'll hang out at the park," Randi began. "Then we'll have lunch at my house—peanut butter and jelly. My favorite."

"Okay," Woody said slowly.

Randi continued. "After lunch we'll make frozen fruit bars from apple juice. *Then* we can go to the town pool for a swim. Mom said she'd take us." Randi paused. "Did you write all that down?"

"Sort of . . . ," Woody mumbled.

Randi thought he sounded a little unhappy.

"What's wrong?" she asked. "Don't you want to go swimming? I guess we could play some more at the park instead. Or we could go to the movies. But I told Kristi that this weekend we want to see that new movie *Space Mutants from Mars* with her. Then we can go to the arcade."

"Randi, I—" Woody began.

"Forrest! Time for your chores!" his mother called. Randi could hear her voice faintly over the phone.

"Listen, I have to go now," Woody told Randi.

"But I haven't finished telling you what we're going to do for the next two weeks," Randi said. "And I haven't even *started* on our plans for the rest of the summer!"

"Forrest! Now!" Mrs. Bowen said. Randi thought she sounded louder this time.

"Sorry," Woody said. "I really have to go. Bye."

Click! He hung up.

Oh, well, Randi thought. *I'll finish telling him all our plans tomorrow while we're at the park. Then he'll be as excited as I am!*

Yup. Randi smiled to herself. *It is going to be one super summer!*

3
Just Like Anna

Randi leaped out of bed. "Good morning!" she said to her little sister, Laurie. "Today is going to be so much *fun!*"

Every day this week has been great, Randi thought. *Hanging out with Woody is just as much fun as hanging out with Anna.*

"Fun!" three-year-old Laurie echoed. She jumped up and down on her bed across the room, holding her stuffed bunny, Nancy.

So far, Randi and Woody had done all sorts of cool things like swimming, riding their bikes, and going to the video arcade at the mall.

Today Randi and Woody were going to do one of their favorite things—in-line skating in the park!

They had been in-line skating *three times* since the summer began!

Randi washed up, brushed her teeth, and pulled on a pair of shorts and a T-shirt. Then she hurried down to the kitchen. Even though it was early, the kitchen was already full of people. Everyone in her huge family was getting ready for breakfast.

The six-year-old twins, Michael and Mark, played under the table with their action figures. Laurie ran around the table in her nightgown. Randi's twelve-year-old pain-in-the-neck brother, Henry, poured himself a glass of orange juice. And ten-year-old Kristi folded the napkins and set them by everyone's place at the table. Mr. Wong was the only one missing. He was already at work, even though it was Saturday.

Randi's mother reached into the cabinet for a stack of dishes. "Hello, Randi," she called, smiling. "Would you like to make the pancakes this morning?"

"Sure!" Randi said. Everyone was expected to help out in the Wong family. And making pancakes was one of Randi's favorite jobs. Her mom had just taught her how to do it two weeks ago.

Randi pulled a big bowl out of a cabinet. Then she found the pancake mix and a measuring cup. She carefully measured the pancake mix. She was about to pour it into the bowl when someone tugged on her shorts.

Randi glanced down. "Hi, Laurie," she said.

"Can I help?" Laurie asked.

"Okay," Randi said. She let Laurie pour the pancake mix into the bowl.

Then Randi used the measuring cup to measure out some water. Laurie stood up on her tiptoes. "Can I pour the water in?"

"Uh—I guess so," Randi said. She watched her sister carefully pour the water into the bowl.

"Can I mix it? Can I mix it, too?" Laurie asked.

"Laurie, *I'm* supposed to be making the pancakes," Randi complained.

"But I can do it!" Laurie argued.

"No," Randi said. "You're too little. You might mess the pancakes up. Let me do it."

Randi took a fork from the kitchen drawer and stirred the batter quickly. When it was ready, she handed it to her mom.

Mrs. Wong poured circles of batter into the hot

13

skillet on the stove. "What are your plans today, Randi?" she asked as the pancakes sizzled gently.

"I'm going in-line skating with Woody," Randi answered.

"But you don't have any in-line skates," Mrs. Wong said.

"She's using my old pair, Mom," Kristi told her. "They don't fit me anymore."

"Woody and I like to go to Brice Park," Randi said. "It's perfect. It's filled with lots of smooth roads and sidewalks, so we won't trip and fall."

Randi's mom served each of Randi's brothers and sisters a stack of hot pancakes. Everyone in the Wong family liked their pancakes with syrup. Everyone but Randi. She ate hers smothered with strawberry jelly.

Randi licked the last bit of jelly off her fork. She glanced up at the clock over the stove. "Yikes!" she yelled. "I told Woody I'd meet him at the park right now! I'm going to be late!"

She ran out the front door and plopped herself down on the steps. She quickly slipped into her knee and elbow pads and buckled up her skates.

She skated like crazy down the sidewalk toward the park. Once she almost ran into a lady with a shopping cart. She had to drag her heel and stop quickly. That was hard. It was much easier to stop on ice skates!

Soon Randi spied Brice Park's tall trees in front of her. She turned in at the main entrance and headed for the old basketball court.

"Wow! Look at all the people in there," she said to herself. A huge group of boys skated around the court.

Randi grabbed on to the fence to stop. She glanced around. *Where is Woody?* she wondered. *He's late!*

She peered through the wire fence, watching the boys on the court. They were playing a game. It looked like hockey—except that there wasn't any ice.

They're playing roller hockey! Randi realized. The game was a lot like ice hockey. You moved the puck around the court with a stick and tried to shoot it into the other team's goal.

Suddenly Randi caught a flash of red hair on the court.

Hey! Woody's playing roller hockey! she thought. *I wonder why he's doing that when he's supposed to be meeting me.*

"Woody!" she called.

Woody glanced up. He waved his hockey stick at Randi but kept on skating.

Randi plopped down on a park bench to wait for him. She wondered how long the game would last.

The boys zipped around the basketball court. A couple of them seemed really good. *This game looks kind of fun,* Randi thought. *Maybe I can play, too.*

Then someone passed Woody the puck. He lifted his stick and whacked the puck. *Thock!* It flew through the goalie's legs and into the goal.

"*Score!*" Woody yelled. He threw his arms up in the air.

Randi jumped up from the bench. "Yay, Woody!" she shouted.

The other boys patted Woody on the back. Woody called a time-out. He skated over to Randi.

"Hey, you're really good," Randi told him.

"Thanks," Woody said, smiling.

"Can I play the next time?" Randi asked. She couldn't wait to learn roller hockey. It looked like so much fun.

Woody's smile faded. "No, Randi! You can't play hockey!"

"Huh? Why not?" Randi asked.

Woody glanced around the park. "Uh—because you're a girl! And you wouldn't be any good at it," he told her.

Randi stared hard at Woody. "How do you know? You never played hockey with me," she challenged.

"Randi, how many times have you played hockey?" Woody asked.

"Well . . ." Randi kicked a pebble with her skate wheel. "Never, I guess."

Woody smiled. "See! You never played before! So how good can you be?"

Randi frowned. "But—" she began.

"Hey, Woody, let's go!" the goalie called.

Woody skated over to rejoin the game.

Randi sat back down with a thud. *I don't get it,* she thought. *Didn't Woody say we could do every-thing together this summer? Then why can't I try playing roller hockey?*

The game ended a few minutes later. Randi watched Woody and another player high-five each other. "Good game," Randi heard the boy say.

"I had fun," Woody told him.

"Want to play with our team again tomorrow?

We're the Falcons. I'm cocaptain, Tommy Burns," the boy continued. "We're part of the park league. It has six teams that play against each other. The games are every day at noon."

"Cool!" Woody said. "That would be great."

Wait a second! What was Woody saying? Randi jumped up. She tugged on Woody's sleeve.

"You can't play hockey tomorrow, Woody," she whispered to him. "We already have plans, remember? Kristi is taking us to the movies."

"I want to play hockey," Woody whispered back.

"But we already have plans. And *you said* we could hang out together while Anna's away," Randi reminded him.

Woody's cheeks turned pink. He looked at Tommy. "Sorry," he said. "I can't play tomorrow. Randi and I are going to the movies."

Tommy shrugged. "Too bad—maybe some other time." He turned and skated toward the other team members.

Woody watched Tommy as he glided away.

Randi tugged on Woody's elbow. "Come on, let's skate. Then we have to be home by twelve-thirty for grilled cheese sandwiches."

Woody scowled. "I don't like grilled cheese," he said.

Randi rolled her eyes. Why was Woody acting so weird?

"That's because you haven't tried my mom's famous grilled cheese sandwiches." Randi smiled. "You're going to love them. Just like Anna does. Anna and I eat grilled cheese every Saturday during the summer."

Woody didn't say anything. Randi skated off. Then she realized Woody wasn't skating behind her. In fact, he hadn't moved at all.

"Come on, slowpoke!" She laughed. "Let's skate some more before lunch!"

Woody slowly skated up to join her. He was still frowning.

What's his problem? Randi thought. *If he keeps acting weird, my great summer is going to turn into a great big disaster!*

4

Poor Woody!

On Sunday morning, Randi couldn't wait to get dressed and head to the mall. Today she and Woody were going to see *Space Mutants from Mars* with Kristi.

Randi had been watching TV ads about the movie all week. It was in 3-D. That meant everyone in the audience got special glasses. When you wore them, the glasses made everything in the movie seem to pop right out of the screen!

As Randi headed into the kitchen for breakfast, the phone rang. Randi heard her mom answer it.

"Randi," Mrs. Wong called. "It's for you."

Randi took the receiver from her mother. Before she could say hello, Laurie tugged on her shorts.

"Can I talk? Can I?" Laurie asked.

"Not now, Laurie," Randi said impatiently. She put the phone to her ear. "Hello?"

"Hi, it's Woody," a scratchy voice answered.

"Woody? What's wrong? You sound awful," Randi told him.

"I'm sick." Woody coughed loudly. "I can't come to the movies today."

He coughed again, even more loudly this time.

Randi held the phone away from her ear. *Oooh. That sounded bad,* she thought. *Poor Woody!*

Randi sighed. "Too bad you can't come. I bet you would love *Space Mutants from Mars*."

Laurie tugged on Randi's hand. "Can *I* come to the movies with you? *I* want to see *Space Mutants from Mars*."

"No, Laurie. I'm going with Kristi," Randi answered. "Besides, you're too young for such a scary movie. It's only for big kids."

Laurie turned away, pouting.

Randi spoke into the phone again. "Sorry, Woody. Laurie keeps interrupting. I hope you feel better soon."

"Thanks. Bye," Woody croaked. He hung up.

* * *

Randi slurped root beer in Vinny's Pizzeria at the mall. "*Space Mutants from Mars* was great, Kristi," she told her sister. "Thanks for taking me."

"You're welcome," Kristi replied. "I had fun, too."

"Too bad Woody didn't see it. He would have liked the scary parts," Randi said.

"Yeah. Especially the space mutants," Kristi agreed. "They looked like giant fish with legs."

Poor Woody, Randi thought. *No movies. No pizza. Being sick is no fun.*

She pictured him at home. Lying in bed, coughing. She wished she could do something to make him feel better.

"Well, come on," Kristi said, swallowing the last of her root beer. "Let's head over to the arcade."

"Wait!" Randi called. She had a great idea!

She pulled out her change purse and counted up her quarters. "I have three dollars," she announced. "Instead of going to the arcade, let's go buy Woody a get-well present!"

"Okay, if you want to," Kristi said. "Where should we buy it?"

"How about that new store, Sports Sensations?"

"Good idea." Kristi stood up. "Let's go!"

Randi and Kristi took the escalator to the lower level of the mall and walked into Sports Sensations. Randi gazed around in wonder. The store held racks and racks of bikes, skis, tennis rackets, and other sports equipment.

"Wow!" She ran over to one of the displays. "Look at all these in-line skates!"

"Well, what do you want to buy?" Kristi asked.

"Do I have enough money for a new pair of skates?" Randi wondered aloud.

Kristi laughed. "I don't think so. Besides, I thought you wanted to get something for Woody."

"Oh, yeah. Right." Randi left the skate display and began walking around the store.

Hmmm, she thought. *What would be the perfect present for Woody? New wrist guards for in-line skating? No, they cost too much. So do knee pads.*

There was a rack of key chains by the cash register. Randi walked over to check them out. As she got closer, she spotted a red plastic key chain—shaped like an in-line skate!

"That's it!" she cried. "Look, Kristi. It's perfect!"

She turned the key chain over. There was no price tag on it. "How much is this, please?" she asked the woman behind the counter.

"Two dollars and fifty cents," the woman answered.

"You have just enough, Randi," Kristi said.

"Great!" Randi dumped her change purse out onto the counter. "I'll take it!"

After that, Randi and Kristi headed out to the bus. As they rode home, Randi slipped the new key chain out of its bag. She held it up, smiling. *This key chain is sure to make Woody feel better!* she thought.

Randi returned the key chain to the bag. She stared out the bus's open window at the beautiful sunny day.

The bus moved slowly past Brice Park. Randi spotted some boys skating around the old basketball court. She leaned forward.

"Look, Kristi!" she called, pointing. "Those are the boys Woody played roller hockey with yesterday." She leaned out the window to wave. "Hey, guys!"

Kristi grabbed the back of her shorts. "Careful, Randi! You'll fall out!"

"I'll be fine," Randi promised. "Hey, guys! It's me—"

Suddenly she froze. There, in the middle of the crowd of boys—it looked like . . .

"What's wrong?" Kristi asked. "Are you okay?"

Randi hung out the window, staring. "I don't believe it," she said. But she couldn't mistake that red hair.

It was Woody! He wasn't at home feeling sick and awful. He was out!

Out playing roller hockey with the guys!

5

Caught in the Act

"Woody lied to me!" Randi exclaimed. "I can't believe it! He made me think he was sick. Then he went out to play roller hockey! I can't believe I felt sorry for him! I am *so* mad!"

Randi sat in the girls' locker room at the Seneca Hills Ice Arena on Tuesday. She and Kate were changing into their ice skates for their Figure Eights lesson.

"Maybe there's some reason why he was at the park. Maybe he felt better or something," Kate suggested. "Did you talk to him?"

"No. I was too mad to call him," Randi admitted. She laced up her skates quickly. Then she jumped to her feet. "But I'm going to talk to him about it now! I'll see you on the ice, okay?"

Randi pushed open the door of the locker room and marched out to the rink. She stepped onto the ice.

Woody was already there, horsing around with Max and Josh. Randi skated over and tapped him on the shoulder. "I'm glad you're feeling better, Woody," she said.

"Uh . . . ," Woody said. His face turned red. He glanced all around the rink.

Randi narrowed her eyes at him. "You were sick, remember? Hoarse voice? Terrible cough?"

"Oh. Right. That," he said. "Well . . . I'm better! I stayed in bed for two days and now I'm better!"

"You are *such* a liar!" Randi shouted. "I saw you. You were playing roller hockey in the park!"

Woody stared down at his skates. "Uh—that's when I started to feel better. So I went out—for some fresh air."

"I don't believe you," Randi shot back. She stared Woody straight in the eye. "Tell the truth, Woody. You weren't really sick at all, were you?"

"Okay. You're right," Woody admitted. "I lied."

"I knew it!" Randi yelled.

"But I *had* to, Randi," Woody went on. "I really wanted to play roller hockey. But you told me I couldn't. You said we *had* to go the movies. You didn't give me any choice."

"You could have just told me the truth," Randi argued. "You didn't have to lie." She folded her arms and stared at Woody.

"I guess you're right," Woody mumbled. "I—I'm sorry."

Well, at least he's apologizing, Randi thought. *He does look kind of sorry. And I guess I did tell him we had to go see* Space Mutants from Mars.

Maybe she should have let Woody say what *he* wanted to do instead.

Maybe she should have played roller hockey with him.

"Well—it's all right, I guess," she said slowly. Then she smiled. "You missed a good movie."

Woody grinned. "Were the monsters scary?"

"With the 3-D glasses on they were," Randi said. "They looked like they were close enough to reach out and grab you!"

"Wow!" Woody cried. "Hey—want to see it again? With me?"

"Maybe," Randi replied. "But not tomorrow. I have tomorrow all planned out. Remember? We're going to play miniature golf."

Woody's smile faded. "Um . . . that sounds like fun, but—"

"But what?" Randi demanded.

"I told the guys I'd play roller hockey with them tomorrow," Woody said. "They need me. I—uh, I kind of joined the team."

Woody made plans without even talking to me? Randi was about to get mad all over again.

But then she thought of something. If they were going to spend the whole summer together, they should do stuff *Woody* wanted to do every now and then.

"Well, okay," she said. "I guess we could play hockey instead of miniature golf."

A frown crossed Woody's face. "Randi!" he said. "I told you before. You *can't* play. You're not good enough!"

"But . . ." Randi stared at him, hurt. "That's not

fair! How am I supposed to *learn* if you never even let me play?"

Before Woody could answer, Carol Crandall, the Figure Eights' coach, skated out and blew her whistle. It was time for practice to start.

Woody skated off with Max and Josh. Randi stared after him for a second. Then she glided over to where the other Figure Eights skaters waited.

"Let's start by working on our backward sculling today," Carol told the group.

Randi glared across the ice at Woody. He turned away. She could tell he was pretending not to see her.

I'm glad I didn't give him that key chain I bought for him, Randi thought. *He doesn't deserve it. He promised to spend the whole summer with me. Now he's ditching me for this hockey team, and he won't even let me play.*

Woody is going to ruin my whole summer!

6

How to Play Roller Hockey

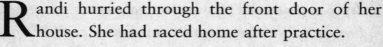

Randi hurried through the front door of her house. She had raced home after practice.

That was because she had a plan. She was going to teach herself to play roller hockey. Then Woody couldn't say she wasn't good enough.

Randi cupped her hands around her mouth. "Henry!" she called. "Where are you?"

Kristi herded the twins, Mark and Michael, down the stairs. "What do you want Henry for?" she asked. "Are you two fighting again?"

"No," Randi answered. "I need to ask him a question. Is he here?"

Kristi shook her head. "He's at his friend James's house."

"Well, I'm borrowing his hockey stick," Randi announced. She ran up the stairs and into Henry's room. She pulled open his closet door.

"Aaaa!" she yelled. Clothes, games, toys, shoes—everything tumbled out of the closet into a big pile. What a mess!

Randi stuck her head into the closet and began sorting through Henry's stuff.

"What are you doing?" a small voice asked.

Randi jumped and spun around. Laurie stood in the doorway.

"Don't sneak up on people like that, Laurie," Randi scolded. She turned back and went on looking through the closet. The hockey stick had to be in there somewhere!

"Okay. What are you doing?" Laurie repeated.

"I'm looking for something," Randi said over her shoulder.

"What are you looking for?"

Randi sighed. Couldn't Laurie leave her alone for once?

"Why don't you go play with Mark and Michael?" she said.

Laurie tugged on Randi's shirt. "I want to play with *you*."

Randi was inside Henry's closet by now. At last she spotted the hockey stick—all the way in the back.

She pulled it out. Then she sorted through the junk on the floor. In a moment she found a hockey puck.

She jammed the rest of Henry's stuff back into the closet. She carried the stick and puck downstairs and out to the porch. Then she put on her in-line skates and skated onto the driveway.

Laurie tagged along after her. She sat on the front steps, watching Randi. "How come you are using Henry's stuff?" Laurie asked.

"Because I want to show Woody I can play roller hockey, just like he can," Randi explained.

She took two empty soda cans from the garage. She set them up on one end of the driveway as the goal. Then she put the puck on the driveway and lowered the stick.

"How hard can it be, anyway?" she said to Laurie. "All you have to do is hit the puck."

Randi swung the stick at the puck.

The puck didn't move.

Randi had missed it!

Laurie laughed. "That was funny!" She giggled.

Randi tried again. She swung the stick with all her might.

This time she hit the puck so hard it flew straight up into the air. That didn't seem right. None of the guys Woody played with ever hit the puck straight up.

Laurie laughed again. Harder this time.

Randi crossed over to the edge of the lawn and picked up the puck. "Hmmm," she said. "Maybe this *is* harder than it looks."

She tried shooting the puck between the two cans. She stared at the goal. Concentrated on it. Then she drew back her stick and swung.

Whack! The puck flew into the air again. It hit the garage door with a crash. It bounced off and flew over Randi's head.

Randi ducked. Just in time.

"What are you trying to do, kill somebody?" a voice shouted from behind her.

Randi turned. Henry stood at the end of the driveway with his friend James.

"Who said you could borrow my hockey stuff?" Henry asked.

"You weren't home, so I couldn't ask you," Randi explained. "I need to learn to play roller hockey. And I need to learn now."

Henry laughed out loud. "*You* want to play hockey? You don't even know how to hold the stick right."

Randi felt her face turn bright red. "Whoops! How *am* I supposed to hold the stick?" she asked.

James stepped forward. "Like this," he said. He took the stick out of Randi's hands. He placed one hand at the top of the stick and one hand closer to the bottom.

"Your hands were too far up," he explained. "If you hold it here, you have more control."

"Oh," Randi said, nodding.

"And don't swing the stick so high when you shoot the puck. That's why it flew into the air last time." James pushed the puck around the driveway, keeping the stick close to the ground. He moved the puck right, then left.

Then, *boom*! He shot it right between the soda cans and into the goal.

"Score!" Randi shouted. She turned to Henry. "Wow! James is really good!"

"*Duh,* he should be," Henry said. "He plays on our school team. We took first place last year."

"That's so cool," Randi said. "Do you play for the league at the park, too?"

"No," James answered. "I'm too old for that league. But some of the younger guys on my school team do. They really love it." He picked up the puck and handed it to Randi.

"James," Randi blurted out. "Would you help me learn how to play roller hockey?"

Henry burst out laughing again.

James ignored him. He handed Randi the hockey stick. "Why don't you start by holding the stick like I showed you," he said.

Randi took the stick and imitated the way James held it. The stick was almost as tall as she was!

"Look at her!" Henry hooted. "Randi, you can't play hockey. You're such a little runt."

"The guys in the park league are my size," Randi snapped. She concentrated on putting her hands in the right position.

"Good," James said. "Now skate up and down the driveway with the stick close to the ground."

On the first few tries, Randi wobbled and stumbled. She wasn't used to skating hunched over. But soon she felt more comfortable. "Now what?" she asked James.

"Now try sliding the puck with the stick while you're skating," he told her. "But just use the front half of the blade to move the puck around."

Randi did what James told her. "Hey!" she said. "I was doing it all wrong! This is much easier!"

Henry tugged on James's elbow. "Come on. Playing with my little sister is boring. Let's go inside and get something to eat." He turned and walked into the house.

"Sure, Henry," James answered. He jogged over to the front door. "Keep practicing," he told Randi.

"Thanks a lot, James," Randi called.

She skated back to the goal. She tried moving the puck up and down the driveway. She concentrated on moving the puck around the right way, but it kept slipping away from her.

"Can I play, Randi?" Laurie called from the steps.

Randi brushed her hair off her forehead. "No. You don't have any skates."

"James didn't have skates on when *he* played. He was wearing sneakers."

"But he was just showing me what to do," Randi explained. "Besides, you're too little to play roller hockey."

Laurie stuck out her bottom lip and frowned.

Randi pushed the puck around with the stick. "I have to practice right now, Laurie. We can play something else later."

Randi bent over the puck again. Out of the corner of her eye she noticed Laurie heading back into the house.

Thank goodness, Randi thought. *Without Laurie bugging me, maybe I can* really *practice.*

She worked on shooting the puck into the goal. And on keeping her stick at the right height.

An hour later, Henry and James came out of the house. They stood at the edge of the driveway and watched Randi.

"Wow," James said. "You're doing well."

Randi grinned. "I've been practicing hard."

"It shows," James told her.

Randi leaned on her hockey stick. "Thanks, but I think I need someone to practice with."

"Don't look at James," Henry said. "He's way too good for you."

"Actually," James admitted, "I could use some help. I need someone to be the goalie when I shoot."

"I can do that!" Randi cried.

"Being goalie is hard, Randi," Henry told her. "Really hard. Think you can handle it?"

Randi smiled. With James's help, she would learn how to play roller hockey really fast. And soon she'd be good enough to play with anyone!

"You bet I can handle it!" she answered her brother.

7

Randi Saves the Day

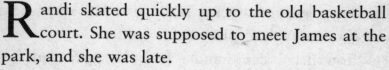

Randi skated quickly up to the old basketball court. She was supposed to meet James at the park, and she was late.

Her mom had asked her to dry the breakfast dishes. And Laurie had wanted to help. Again. When Laurie helped with Randi's chores, they always took more time.

Randi rounded a corner and saw James sitting on the curb. Beside him were a giant duffel bag and a hockey goal.

"Hi," she gasped, trying to catch her breath. "Whoa! That's the biggest duffel bag I've ever seen."

"It's got all my old equipment in it from when I used to play goalie," James explained. "My mom dropped me off so I wouldn't have to walk here with all this stuff."

He reached into the bag and pulled out a white helmet with a wire face guard. "This is a goalie's mask. Try it on."

Randi lifted the helmet onto her head. It was really heavy. And when she peered through the face guard, she felt as if she were behind a big fence.

"What's this wire part for?" she asked.

"Protection," James explained. "You don't want to get hit in the face with a flying hockey puck."

Randi pushed the face guard up and peered into James's bag. It was filled with big white pads.

"You need to wear all these, too. They'll keep you from getting hurt if the puck hits you," James explained. "Try them on." He helped Randi into the chest and shoulder pads first. Then he put a giant red-and-blue jersey on over them. Next he strapped long pads onto Randi's legs.

Randi tried to skate forward. "My body feels like it's in cement. And how am I supposed to see out of this mask?"

"Hold on. You're not done yet," James said. He reached into the bag again and held out two huge gloves. "The blocking pad goes on your right arm, and the catching glove goes on your left hand," he explained.

When she finally had all the equipment on, Randi wobbled up and down the court. *Boy,* she thought. *This is hard. And I feel pretty silly.*

"Ready to try some shots?" James asked. "You be the goalie, and I'll try to shoot past you. All you have to do is stand in front of the goal and stop the puck. Then hit it away from me."

"Uh—okay," Randi said. "Let's go for it."

James skated up the court with the puck, then turned around.

Yikes! Here he comes! Randi thought.

James swerved to the right and shot the puck at the goal.

Randi saw the puck speeding toward her. She squeezed her eyes closed and threw her hands up in front of her face.

"Score!" James cried.

Randi opened her eyes. *Where did the puck go?* she wondered. She turned around to look behind her.

The puck sat in the goal.

"Oops," she said, blushing.

"That's okay," James said. "Try again. But this time *block* the puck. Don't be afraid of it. Think of all the padding you have on. The puck can't hurt you."

James took the puck down the court again. He turned and sped back toward Randi. He shot!

The puck flew toward Randi—and the goal. She held her stick out.

Whack! The puck hit her stick and stopped dead.

"I did it!" she squealed.

"Hey, that's pretty good," James said. "Now try this one."

His shot went into the air. Randi stuck her padded arm out to block it.

It worked! The puck hit the padding and fell to the ground.

Randi and James kept practicing. Randi blocked as many shots as she could. The longer they practiced, the better she got!

"This is *totally* fun!" she told James.

He smiled at her. "You're pretty good. I can't believe you never played goalie before!"

Randi glanced up. A couple of members of Woody's team, the Falcons, were skating past. One of them was Tommy, the boy who had invited Woody to play.

The boys stood to the side and watched Randi and James practicing. Randi gulped and tried to forget they were there.

"James!" Tommy called after a few minutes. "Who's that with you?"

"Hi, Tommy. Hi, Jonathan. That's Randi," James told him.

"He's pretty good," Tommy said.

Randi grinned with pride—then stopped short.

Wait a second. I'm not a "he." I'm a "she," she thought.

They think I'm a boy! My helmet is hiding my braids. And my name could be a boy's name. That's pretty funny!

Tommy skated over to James. "Can we practice with you guys?"

"Okay with you?" James asked Randi.

Randi nodded.

"Great!" Tommy said.

Randi took her place in the goal. James, Tommy, and Jonathan began passing the puck back and forth among them.

Bam! Jonathan shot the puck.

Randi stuck out her stick and stopped it. She hit it off to the side, the way James had told her to.

"Nice save," Jonathan called.

Totally cool! Randi thought. *I wish Woody could see me now. Then he couldn't say I wasn't good enough!*

They played a little while longer. Then James stopped the game. "I have to go now. My mom's picking me up soon," he said.

"This is fun," Tommy declared. He turned to Randi. "You're a great goalie. Too bad you don't play for the Falcons."

"Yeah, we need a good goalie," Jonathan chimed in. "Our regular one is going on vacation in a couple of days. We don't have anyone to replace him. *And* we have a big game coming up."

"It's against the Cougars. They were the only team that beat us last year," Tommy explained.

"Hey! Maybe Randi could fill in for the goalie," James suggested.

Randi's heart began to pound. Were they serious? Did they really want to put her in a game?

"Why not?" Tommy said. "Can you do it, Randi?"

Randi didn't know what to say. Was she really ready to play for a team?

"Sure! Randi can do it," James answered for her. He put his hand on Randi's shoulder. "Want to?"

Randi still didn't answer. But not because she wasn't sure. Because she was thinking hard. Because she was starting to get a great idea. . . .

Woody's on the Falcons, she thought. *We'll be on the same team, but I won't tell him I'm playing goalie. He'll think I'm a boy, just like Tommy and Jonathan do!*

I'll play a great game—then I'll show Woody it was really me in the goal! He'll be so surprised! He'll have to admit I was good enough! And he'll learn his lesson.

Randi nodded at Tommy and Jonathan. "Okay," she said in her deepest voice. "I'll play for the Falcons!"

8
Randi's Big Secret

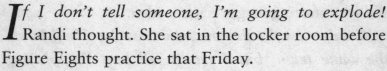

If I don't tell someone, I'm going to explode! Randi thought. She sat in the locker room before Figure Eights practice that Friday.

It had been two days since Tommy had invited Randi to join the Falcons. And Randi hadn't told one person! Normally she would have talked it over with Anna and Woody. But Anna was at camp. And Woody—well, Woody was the one person she *couldn't* tell!

As Randi laced up her skates, someone tapped her shoulder. "Hi, Randi," someone said.

Randi turned around. "Hi, Kate!"

"Let's warm up together," Kate suggested, pulling Randi to her feet.

"Sure," Randi said. She and Kate made their way onto the ice. They skated around the edge of the rink.

Hmmm, Randi thought. *Maybe I can tell Kate. . . .*

"Can you keep a secret?" she blurted out.

Kate blinked. "Uh, I guess so."

"It's a big one. You have to cross your heart and promise you won't tell," Randi said.

Kate's eyes grew big. "I promise. What is it?"

"Remember when I told you that Woody said I wasn't good enough to play hockey with his team?" Randi asked.

"Yeah," Kate replied.

"Well, I *joined* the team!" Randi whispered.

A confused look crossed Kate's face. "Huh? I don't get it."

Randi explained about practicing with James. About how Tommy and Jonathan thought she was a boy. *And* about being invited to play goalie for the Falcons at their next big game!

"Wow, Randi!" Kate said, stunned. "Being a goalie is supposed to be hard. Do you really think you can do it?"

"I think so," Randi answered. "I've been practicing a lot."

Just then Woody and Josh glided by.

"You should see our team, Josh," Randi heard Woody brag. "We're called the Falcons. The only team that has beaten us so far is the Cougars. We play them this weekend."

"Do you think you'll win?" Josh asked.

"Easy," Woody answered. "Especially since we've got a new goalie. I heard he's even better than our regular one!"

Randi clapped her hand over her mouth to stop herself from laughing. Kate did the same thing.

Woody was talking about *Randi*—and he didn't even know it!

"Watch this," Randi whispered to Kate. She skated up to Woody. "Hey, Woody. Did you know I've been practicing roller hockey?"

Woody wrinkled his nose. "So what? I already told you, Randi. You're not good enough."

"But I'm practicing really hard—and I think I'm getting really good," Randi said.

"It doesn't matter. You can't possibly be good

enough to play on my team. *The end!*" Woody shouted. He started to skate away.

"But—" Randi began.

Woody stuck his fingers in his ears. "I'm not listening to you."

"Well, don't worry," Randi shouted. *"I'm never talking to you again!"* She grabbed Kate's arm and they skated away.

"That Woody makes me so mad," she told Kate, her voice shaking. "How could he be so—so *dumb*?"

"Don't worry, Randi," Kate said. "You'll show him. Just wait till the big game."

Randi heard Carol blow her whistle. All the Figure Eights skaters glided over to their coach.

"Okay, everyone," Carol said. "Let's try some pairs work today."

There were excited whispers from the class. In pairs skating, the boys supported the girls in difficult lifts and turns.

No one in Figure Eights had tried a pairs move yet. Pairs skating took a lot of concentration. And you really had to trust your partner not to drop you or let go of you.

Carol glanced at the skaters. "Josh, you work with Kate. Max, you're with Samantha. Randi, you work with Woody."

Oh, no! Randi thought. *Not Woody!* Her stomach squeezed into knots. She skated quickly over to Carol.

"Do I have to skate with Woody?" Randi asked in a low voice.

"I paired everyone up by size and strength," Carol explained. "You and Woody are best suited for each other. Anyway, I thought Woody was one of your best friends."

"Not anymore," Randi replied. "Now he's my *worst* friend."

Carol glanced over at the rest of the group. "I'm sorry, but I'm afraid you have to skate with him, Randi. At least for this lesson."

Carol leaned closer to Randi. She put her hand on Randi's shoulder. "Don't worry," she said with a smile. "Sometimes friends fight. But I'm sure you two will make up."

"Not this time," Randi muttered under her breath.

"Okay, pair up, everyone," Carol instructed the group.

Randi skated back over to Woody. She stood beside him. But she didn't look at him.

"Now face your partner and hold hands," Carol went on. "Girls, you will stretch your right leg out behind you. Boys, your job is to gently scull backward so that you pull your partner along. Watch. I'll show you how."

Carol skated over to Samantha. She took her hands. Samantha lifted her leg behind her. She leaned forward, putting all her weight on Carol's hands. As Carol glided backward, she pulled Samantha with her.

That looks beautiful, Randi thought. *I can't wait to try it! If only I could practice it with someone besides Woody . . .*

"Thanks, Samantha." Carol smiled and turned to the group. "Okay, guys, now you give it a try."

Randi and Woody turned—and scowled at each other. Randi reached out for Woody's hands. He drew them back.

"Woody, come on! You're supposed to hold me up!" Randi said. She grabbed Woody's hands, balanced on one leg, and leaned her weight on him.

But his hands felt limp, not strong. Randi felt herself falling forward. Her legs slipped out from under her.

"*Oh, no!*" she yelped.

Splat! She fell on the ice, landing on her knees.

"Ow!" Randi glared up at Woody. "You did that on purpose!"

"I did not," he protested. "I just wasn't ready."

Carol skated up. "Randi, are you okay?" She reached down and pulled Randi to her feet.

Randi rubbed her knees. "Yes."

"Why don't you go to the side and rest for a minute?" Carol said. "Woody can work with me."

"I'd like that better," Woody muttered.

"Me too!" Randi shouted over her shoulder.

"What happened?" Kate called as Randi skated past.

"Woody let me fall—on purpose!" Randi glared back at him. "He wanted to make me look stupid in front of everyone. But just wait. He's going to be sorry after we win our game on Friday. Then *he'll* be the one who looks stupid!"

9

The Big Game

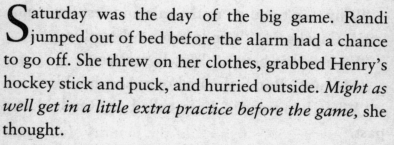

Saturday was the day of the big game. Randi jumped out of bed before the alarm had a chance to go off. She threw on her clothes, grabbed Henry's hockey stick and puck, and hurried outside. *Might as well get in a little extra practice before the game,* she thought.

As she skated up and down the driveway with her stick and puck, she thought about her plan. If everything went the way it was supposed to, Woody would have to admit he was wrong. That she *was* good enough to play with the team.

But what if everything *didn't* go the way it was supposed to?

What if Randi had a bad game?

What if—because of her—the Falcons lost?

Randi's stomach twisted. If Anna had been there, the two of them could have discussed the plan. That would have made Randi feel much better.

"Randi! Breakfast!" Mrs. Wong called.

Randi hurried into the kitchen, washed her hands, and slid into her seat. She gobbled down her first stack of pancakes. Then a second. She wanted to be sure she had plenty of energy!

"My," Mrs. Wong said. "You have a big appetite today."

Randi gulped the last of her milk. "Yep," she said, wiping away her milk mustache. "I'm in a big hockey game today at noon in Brice Park."

"Sounds fun," Randi's mom said. "Before you leave, please be sure to fold the laundry. It's in the basket on the dryer."

"Okay, Mom." Randi took her plate to the sink and then found the laundry basket. It was so full she could barely see over the top. She carried it to the family room sofa and plopped it down in front of her.

She began folding. T-shirts first. Then shorts. Then underwear and socks.

59

Laurie poked her head around the side of the sofa. "What are you doing?" she asked.

"Folding laundry," Randi answered.

Laurie edged closer. "Can I help?"

Randi sighed. "Not now, Laurie. I don't have much time, and I have to do this right."

"Why can't I try?" Laurie asked.

Randi frowned. Laurie was being such a pest. Did she have to do *everything* Randi did?

"T-shirts are hard to fold," Randi explained. She held one up against Laurie. "See? This one's bigger than you! How could you ever fold it? You're way too little."

Laurie flopped down beside Randi on the sofa.

Randi glanced at her little sister. Laurie stuck her bottom lip out in a pout. She stared down at the floor.

I didn't mean to make Laurie sad, Randi thought. *Maybe I can explain why I won't let her help.*

"Look, Laurie," she began. "I'm sorry you're upset. But every time I'm home, you want to do things with me."

"What's wrong with that?" Laurie asked.

"Nothing," Randi said. "Except that I can't do

things with you *every minute* of the day. Sometimes I want to do things by myself—or with someone else."

"You don't *like* doing stuff with me?" Laurie asked, sticking her bottom lip out even farther.

"No. That's not what I meant. I love you, Laurie. And I like spending time with you," Randi declared. "I just need to do things with other people. Do you understand?"

Laurie looked up at Randi. "I think so," she said.

Randi gave her sister a hug. "Good."

Then, out of the corner of her eye, Randi caught a glimpse of the clock. "Yikes! It's eleven-thirty! I'm supposed to stop by James's house before the game! I'd better run!"

Randi quickly finished up the laundry. She gave Laurie another hug and said, "I promise—you and I will do something totally fun together tomorrow."

"Yay!" Laurie yelled.

Randi skated toward the park, loaded down with all her goalie pads. She had put them on at James's house. She had to be sure her disguise was in place before Woody saw her.

In the park, the Falcons were already warming up. Woody skated with Tommy. The two of them passed the puck between them.

Suddenly Randi couldn't move. *What if Woody recognizes me?* she thought. *What if he tells Tommy I'm not a good player? Maybe this is a bad idea. Maybe I should forget the whole—*

"Hey, Randi! Come on!"

Randi glanced up, startled. She saw Tommy waving her over.

I can't back out now, Randi realized. She skated over to the team.

"This is the goalie I was telling you about," Tommy said to Woody. "His name is Randi."

Randi lowered her eyes. She felt her heart pounding in her chest. Would Woody recognize her?

"Hi, I'm Woody," he said. "Glad you're on the team."

He *didn't* recognize her! Randi smiled behind her mask. She nodded at Woody and skated over to the goal.

Yay! she thought. *The first part of my plan went fine.* Then she gulped. *Now all I have to worry about is being a good goalie!*

She felt her stomach tighten up again. Could she do it?

She took her position. As soon as she was settled, the Falcons began to practice taking shots.

Randi stayed alert. She moved fast. But the first two shots got past her for a goal.

Randi groaned. This didn't look good.

But as she began to warm up, she blocked more and more of the Falcons' shots.

A moment later, the Cougars skated onto the other end of the court to warm up. Randi could hear their players taking fast, hard shots at the goal. *Whack! Whack!*

It wouldn't be easy to block *those* shots!

Finally the referee called to the teams. He blew a whistle, signaling that the game was about to start.

The Falcons huddled together. They joined their hands in the middle of the circle. "Go, Falcons!" they cried. Randi only mouthed the words. She didn't want Woody to hear her voice and recognize it.

A group of people gathered around the court to watch.

Randi took her place in the goal. Her palms began to sweat. Her heart thumped in her chest.

The Falcons and Cougars squared off. The referee dropped the puck, and the Falcons snatched it away. Tommy and Jonathan moved the puck down the court toward the Cougars' goal.

Whack! Tommy shot at the goal and missed. A Cougar snagged the puck. He headed back up the court—charging right toward Randi!

She braced herself. This was it! This was the real thing!

The Cougar lifted his stick and shot. The puck flew across the ground.

Randi stuck out her stick and stopped the puck dead. She knocked it off to the side.

Whew! Randi breathed a sigh of relief. *I did it!*

The Falcons tried to score again—but missed. The Cougars snatched the puck and headed back toward Randi.

All the Cougars and Falcons raced down to the goal. Randi tried to keep her eye on the puck, but she couldn't follow it in the crowd. She felt a jolt of panic. *Where's the puck? I can't find it! There are too many people in the way!*

The puck whizzed past Randi and flew into the goal.

"Score!" The Cougars cheered.

Randi stared at the puck in the net behind her. She felt awful.

"No big deal, Randi," Tommy called. "You'll get it next time."

The teams squared off again. Soon the Cougars were racing toward the goal. But this time Randi was ready. The players crowded around her goal, but Randi didn't let the knocking and pushing get in her way.

Whack! Whack! She blocked two shots in a row. The people watching the game cheered. Randi sent the puck flying toward the other end of the court.

"Nice playing," Woody shouted. Randi smiled to herself.

Yes! she thought. *I really* can *play this game!*

Soon the score was tied, 1–1. It stayed even for a very long time. Then Tommy shot the puck into the Cougars' goal and scored another point.

All right! Randi thought. *We're winning!*

"Two minutes left," yelled the scorekeeper.

The Cougars raced the puck down toward Randi's goal.

Stay calm, she coached herself. She kept her eyes on the puck and tried to focus.

Whap! One of the Cougars shot at the goal. The puck came flying through the air. Randi reached out her big catching glove.

Don't lose it! she told herself. *Don't lose it!*

Wham! The puck slapped into her glove pocket.

I caught it! Randy realized.

She tossed the puck as far as she could down to the other end of the court.

Then the whistle blew. "Game over!" the referee yelled.

"We won!" one of the Falcons screamed.

Randi's teammates surrounded her. Everyone crowded around, giving high fives, jumping up and down.

I did it! Randi thought. *I saved the game!*

Now it's time for my surprise. Now I'll show Woody who I really am.

Randi glanced up. Woody stood right in front of her. He laughed and cheered with the rest of the team.

Randi put her hand on the bottom of her goalie mask and slipped it off. Her braids spilled out.

"Surprise, Woody!" she yelled.

Woody turned and stared at Randi. He stopped laughing. His mouth fell open.

"Randi!" he gasped. "I—I don't believe it!"

Boy, Randi thought. *He sure does look surprised!*

"See, Woody?" she said. "I was a great goalie. I told you I could play hockey. I—"

"Hey!" Tommy called, skating over to Randi. "You're a *girl*! I thought Randi was a boy's name."

"It's both," Randi explained.

Woody's face turned beet red. He clenched his fists. He stepped closer to Randi. "Why did you do this?" he yelled.

Randi stared. Woody seemed really angry. "I was just trying to show you that I can play roller hockey too—" she began.

Woody shook his head. "Forget it!" he said, cutting her off. "Just forget everything!"

Then he grabbed his hockey stick and skated away.

10

Learning Your Lesson

Randi watched Woody skate away. *This is not what I planned at all,* she thought. *I didn't mean to make Woody so angry!*

"What's he mad about?" Tommy asked.

"I don't know," Jonathan answered. "Randi played great!"

"Thanks, guys," Randi said. "But I'd better go find out what's wrong. I'll see you later."

She skated after Woody. She caught up to him a block away from the park. "Woody!" she called.

"What do you want?" he snapped.

"I'm sorry you're mad," Randi said. "But I only meant to play a little trick on you. I wanted to get you back for saying I wasn't good enough to play for your team. I practiced really hard, Woody. And you didn't even care!"

"You don't get it, do you?" Woody yelled. "I don't care how much you practiced—or how good you got. I just didn't want to play roller hockey with *you*!"

Randi felt as if Woody had just punched her. "You didn't want to play roller hockey with me? Why?" she asked.

"Because ever since Anna went away to camp, we've been doing *everything* together! You planned out my entire summer. You tried to take over my whole life!" Woody told her.

Randi blinked. Was it true? Had she really tried to take over Woody's life? "But—But you promised you'd hang out with me all summer," she reminded him.

"I know. And I really wanted to. But you wanted me to do all the things you and Anna like to do. And eat the things you and Anna like to eat. Then you wanted me to spend *every minute* with you—like Anna does.

"But I'm not Anna, I'm Woody. And I don't want to do *everything* with you," he continued. "I want to do some things on my own—like play roller hockey. I tried to tell you I wanted to join the team by myself, but I knew you wouldn't listen."

Randi felt confused. And hurt. "But . . . I thought you *liked* doing things with me."

"I do," Woody told her. "But not *everything*. Not every single minute."

Just then Randi thought of Laurie—about how her little sister had been acting. She followed Randi around everywhere. She wanted to do whatever Randi was doing. It was really annoying.

Oh, no! she realized. *I'm doing the same thing to Woody!*

But still, it's not all *my fault. . . .*

"You should have told me I was being too pushy," she argued. "If you'd told me, I would have stopped."

"No, you wouldn't have," Woody said. "I tried to tell you I didn't want grilled cheese for lunch. But you made me eat it anyway! And I *hate* grilled cheese."

Suddenly Randi realized that Woody was right. She had behaved horribly. Woody didn't want someone smothering him all the time. Or someone telling him what to do every second. And that was exactly what she had been doing.

"Wow," she said. "I didn't realize how I was acting. I'm really sorry."

Woody scraped the front wheel of his skate against the ground. "I'm sorry, too, Randi," he said. "I didn't want to hurt your feelings. But I guess I should have been honest with you."

"Look—I'm tired of fighting with you," Randi said slowly. "Do you—Do you think we can be friends again? I promise, I won't try to hang out with you every minute. Really."

Woody stopped and thought. "Yeah," he finally said. "We can be friends again."

Then he smiled. "By the way, you did a really great job as goalie today. I bet the guys will ask you to join the team for the rest of the summer."

"Really?" Randi asked.

"Yeah," Woody answered. "So are you going to join?"

"I don't think so," Randi said. She slung an arm around Woody's shoulders. "If I did, we might end up spending every day together. And then I'd get really sick of you!"

If you glided right through

jump into the SILVER BLADES series, featuring
Randi Wong's big sister Jill and her friends.

Look for these titles at your bookstore or library:

BREAKING THE ICE
IN THE SPOTLIGHT
THE COMPETITION
GOING FOR THE GOLD
THE PERFECT PAIR
SKATING CAMP
THE ICE PRINCESS
RUMORS AT THE RINK
SPRING BREAK
CENTER ICE
A SURPRISE TWIST
THE WINNING SPIRIT
THE BIG AUDITION
NUTCRACKER ON ICE
RINKSIDE ROMANCE
A NEW MOVE
ICE MAGIC
A LEAP AHEAD
MORE THAN FRIENDS
WEDDING SECRETS
NATALIA COMES TO AMERICA
THE ONLY WAY TO WIN

and coming soon:
RIVAL ROOMMATES

About the Author

Effin Older is the author of many children's books published in the United States and abroad.

Effin lived in New Zealand for fourteen years. She currently lives in a tiny village in Vermont with her husband, Jules, and her white husky, Sophie. She has twin daughters named Amber and Willow.

When Effin isn't writing children's books, she likes to take long walks with Sophie, ride her mountain bike, and cross-country ski.